STAR WARS®

THE CLONE WARS™

Instruction Manual

PRESS OUT 'N' BUILD

Construct your very own Clone Wars model collection with this building kit book. Make a clone trooper helmet large enough to wear and a replica of R2-D2 that has a spinning head! Then, tackle the mammoth task of building the AT-TE walker! Read through the instructions before you start and make sure you follow all of the directions and diagrams carefully.

Everything you need to make the models is in this kit, but you might need something to help you pop out some of the smaller card pieces or to help you push tabs into place. A pencil should suffice. You might also want some string, so you can wear your clone trooper helmet.

THE BASICS

When you're ready to start, take out the cards that correspond to the model you are making. So you don't mess up the pieces, only press each one out when the instructions tell you to. As you press out each piece, fold along the scored edges, keeping the printed parts of the model on the outer side. The outside of the model is colored light gray in the diagrams and the inside is dark gray. Clip the pieces of each model together by pushing the tabs through the holes. The tab ends should spring back, locking the pieces in place.

Let the building commence . . .

THE LEVELS:

Begin with Level 1: Padawan—the clone trooper helmet—as this is the easiest model to make. As you work your way through the book, the difficulty level increases, so leave the AT-TE walker until last.

R2-D2 is slightly more complicated, so this is Level 2: Jedi Knight. Look closely at the diagrams to make sure you have everything the right way up and all the pieces should slot into place!

The AT-TE walker model in Level 3 is for budding Jedi Masters. It is the most difficult of the models and you may need some help from your friends or an adult. Are you up for the challenge?

LEVEL 1: PADAWAN

Level 1: Padawan

Your mission in order to reach the Padawan level is to make a clone trooper helmet. Follow these instructions very carefully. If you want to make this into a helmet for yourself, you will also need some string to hold it onto your head. May the Force guide you!

Step 1

Press out pieces 1 and 2. Fold the corners of the tabs in and push the tab on piece 1 into the slot of piece 2 and vice versa, as per the diagrams. This will make the front of the helmet.

FRONT

1
2

BACK

2
1

CLONE TROOPER HELMET

Step 2

Press out piece 3, which is the top of the helmet. Slot it onto the top of pieces 1 and 2 by pushing the middle tabs in first. Then, bend the mask into shape and insert the rest of the tabs from piece 3 into the helmet.

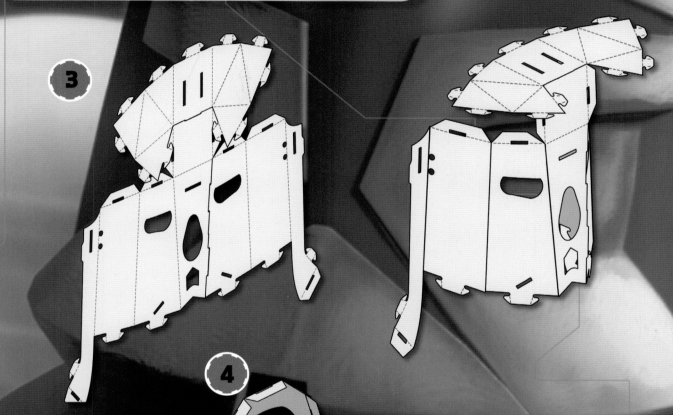

Step 3

Press out piece 4 and slot the tabs from piece 3 into the slots. This acts as a reinforcing rib.

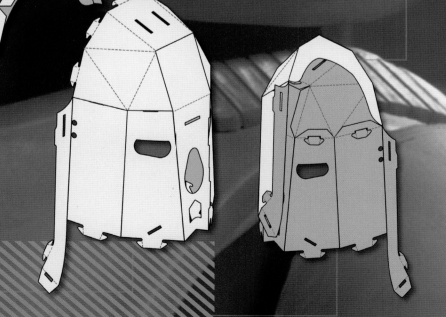

Step 4

Press out piece 5, bend the middle section over and slot the top two tabs into the slots, as shown. Then secure it to piece 3 on the top of the helmet.

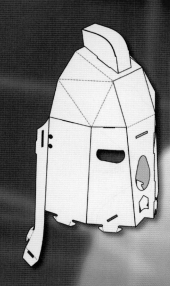

Step 5

Press out pieces 6 and 7 and attach the first tab on piece 6 to piece 7. Then, connect the two pieces with the rest of the tabs to form the neck piece. Finally, connect the neck piece to the four bottom side tabs on the helmet.

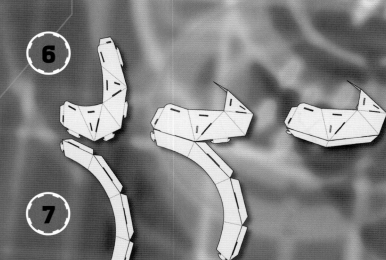

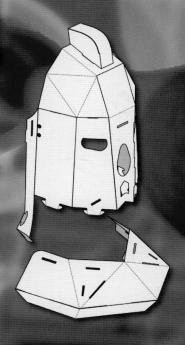

CLONE TROOPER HELMET

Step 6

Press out piece 8. This forms the faceplate of the helmet. Fasten it to the neck section, then connect the triangular side sections, and finally, connect the tab at the top.

Step 7

NOTE: You will need two pieces of string for this step.

Thread pieces of string through the holes on either side of the helmet and tie a knot by the mask to secure it. Put the helmet on your head and tie both pieces of string together at the back.

8

Step 8

To finish, bend the ends of the faceplate (piece 8) around the sides of the helmet and attach the tabs to the ear flaps.

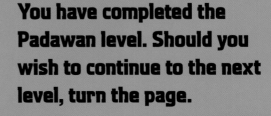

You have completed the Padawan level. Should you wish to continue to the next level, turn the page.

LEVEL 2: JEDI KNIGHT

Level 2: Jedi Knight

Your next mission is to construct a model of R2-D2 with a working spinning head. Complete each step in the correct order and think wisely.

Step 1

Press out piece 1 of R2-D2 and fold it together, slotting the three tabs into place to form his middle leg.

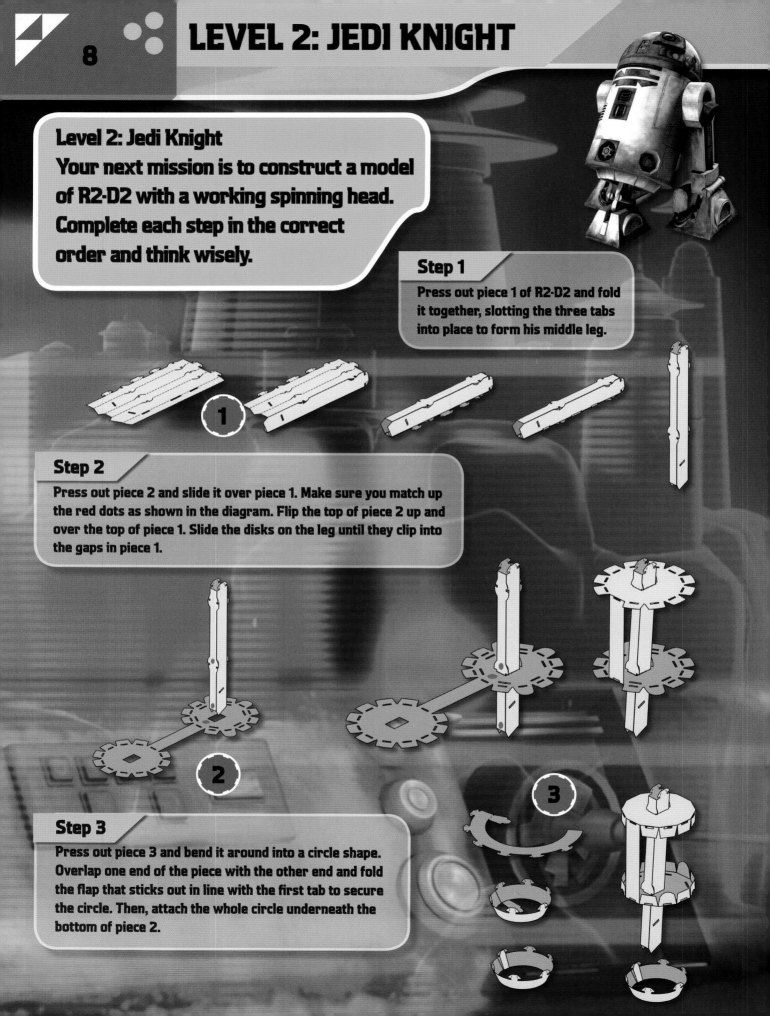

1

Step 2

Press out piece 2 and slide it over piece 1. Make sure you match up the red dots as shown in the diagram. Flip the top of piece 2 up and over the top of piece 1. Slide the disks on the leg until they clip into the gaps in piece 1.

2

3

Step 3

Press out piece 3 and bend it around into a circle shape. Overlap one end of the piece with the other end and fold the flap that sticks out in line with the first tab to secure the circle. Then, attach the whole circle underneath the bottom of piece 2.

Step 4

Press out piece 4. This forms R2-D2's body. Line up the vents in the middle of his body, so they match the vents on piece 2. Starting with the middle, where the vents are, push the tabs in both the top and bottom slots of the model. Then, work your way around fastening the rest of the tabs.

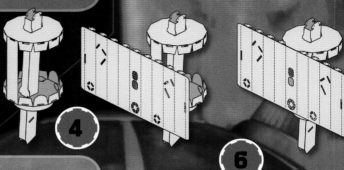

Step 5

Press out pieces 5 and 6. Push piece 5 down over the top of the model until it clicks into place and fold up the edge tabs. It should spin freely. Then, fasten piece 6 into place onto the tabs on piece 1. The red arrows should point forward.

Step 6

Press out piece 7, which forms R2-D2's dome. Locate the red arrow and line it up with the corresponding arrow on piece 5. Fasten the two pieces together and bend piece 7 over the top of the model. Then, bend each segment down individually and fit them in place. Make sure piece 7 is on the outside of piece 5.

Step 7

Press out R2-D2's eyepiece, piece 8, and slot it into place on the dome section as shown.

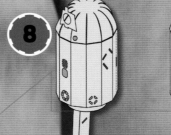

LEVEL 2: JEDI KNIGHT

Step 8

Press out piece 9 and fold it up to make R2's foot. Slot in all of the tabs and attach it to its leg.

Step 9

Press out pieces 10 and 11. These will make R2's left and right legs. Bend these parts into tubes, by slotting in the two side tabs and the one on top.

Step 10

a. Press out pieces 12 and 13. These are the shoulder sections. Slide them over the three connecting tags on the leg sections and fasten the first bottom tab. Then, fold them around the top of the leg and down the other side, fastening the second tab.

b. Bend the side pieces down and tab them in place. Tuck the ends into the last slot and flip the locking tabs over the top, locating them in the same slots. The tabs on pieces 12 and 13 should be tucked inside 10 and 11.

Step 11

Press out pieces 14 and 15 and attach them to the bottom of the legs with the two tabs.

R2-D2

Step 12

Press out pieces 16 and 17. These will make the left and right feet. Fold them into shape, then attach them to the leg sections. Once secured, flip the front and back pieces into place.

17

16

Step 13

Press out pieces 18 and 19 and fold them over, so their tabs fit in the slots, as shown. Then, plug them into R2's feet.

19

18

Step 14

Attach the legs to either side of the body, using the three tabs on each one.

Step 15

Finally, press out piece 20, which is the back plate. First, fasten it to the top and bottom tabs of the body, then slot in the two side tabs.

20

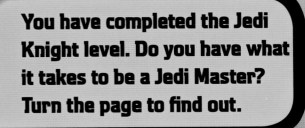

You have completed the Jedi Knight level. Do you have what it takes to be a Jedi Master? Turn the page to find out.

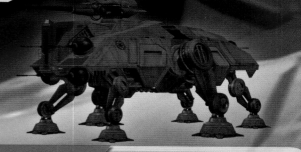

Level 3: Jedi Master
Your final mission is to build a mighty AT-TE walker. Use the diagrams to guide your every move and think only like a true Jedi Master.
May the Force be with you!

Step 1
a. Press out pieces 1–5—these form the body of the walker. Fold down the tabs on piece 1.
b. Turn piece 3 upside down and slot it into the tabs on piece 1 along the bottom.
c. Slot pieces 4 and 5 along the top and sides of piece 1. Then, slot the tabs of panel 2 to the other side to create the body shape.

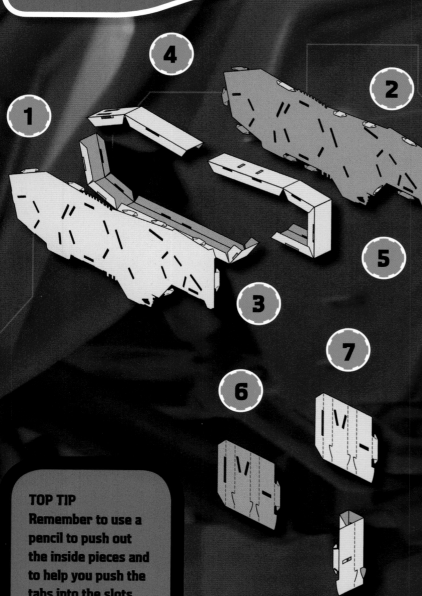

TOP TIP
Remember to use a pencil to push out the inside pieces and to help you push the tabs into the slots.

AT-TE WALKER

Step 2

To make the middle pair of legs:

a. Press out pieces 6 and 7. Fold and fasten them into box shapes. (See diagram on previous page.)

b. Press out pieces 8 and 9 and slide them over the top of the two box shapes.

c. Press out pieces 10-13, which form the soles of the feet. Push the six tabs on pieces 10 and 12 through the six slots on 11 and 13.

d. Take the previously built foot sections and connect the six tabs on each one to the sole sections.

Step 3

To make the shoulder and leg section:

a. Press out pieces 14 and 15—these form the right and left legs. Fold the sides of each one over and slot them together as shown.

b. Press out pieces 16-19 and attach them to the back and front of pieces 14 and 15.

c. Fasten the top of pieces 16 and 17 over the top of the legs.

d. Attach pieces 16 and 17 onto the feet you made earlier and fold over 18 and 19 to fasten.

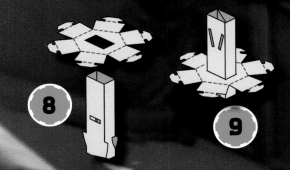

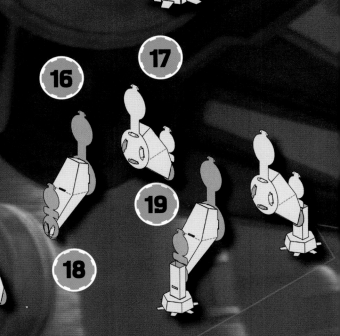
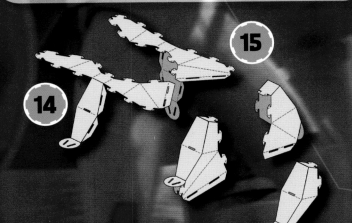

Step 4

Press out pieces 20 and 21 and fasten them to the legs. These form the hubs that attach the legs to the body. Then, fasten the legs to either side of the body.

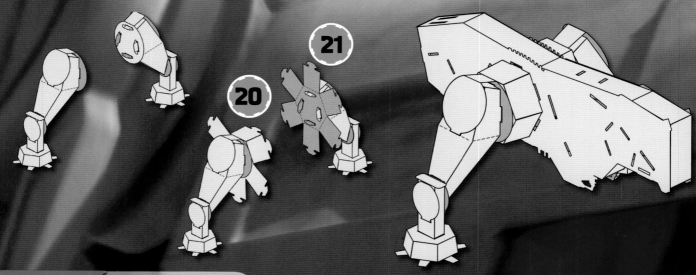

Step 5

To make the back feet:
a. Press out pieces 22 to 29 and assemble them as per the foot section in Step 2 on page 13.
b. Press out pieces 30 and 31—these form the ankle bearing. Slot the two tabs in the slots on each foot as shown.

AT-TE WALKER

Step 6

To make the back legs:

a. Press out pieces 32 and 33, which form the back right leg, and pieces 34 and 35, the back left leg.

b. Fold in the bottom three sides of piece 32—these are the sides with slots, not tabs. Then, fold in the top three sides of piece 33.

c. Place the two halves together and bend in the sides with tabs on them. Where a tab corresponds to a slot, fasten it in place. This should make a leg section with three tabs sticking out of the top and two tabs sticking out of the bottom.

d. Repeat the steps *a* to *c* for pieces 34 and 35.

32 **33** **34** **35**

Step 7

a. Press out piece 36. This will form the back axle. Fold it up as shown, fastening the two tabs.

b. Then, fold the sections into a tube shape and push the remaining six tabs into either side of the back of the body, by wrapping it around.

c. Once the back is secure, plug the feet into the legs and plug the legs into the axle.

36

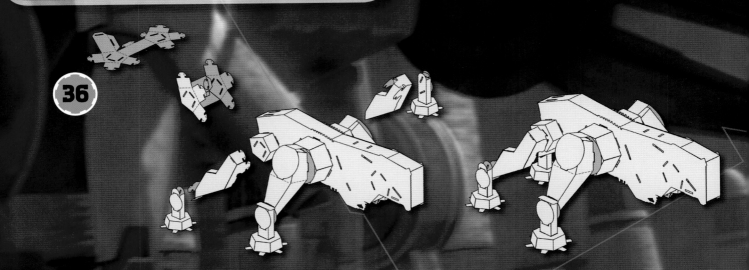

Step 8

To make the front legs:
Press out pieces 37 to 50. Assemble
them in the same way as the back
legs in Step 6 on page 15.

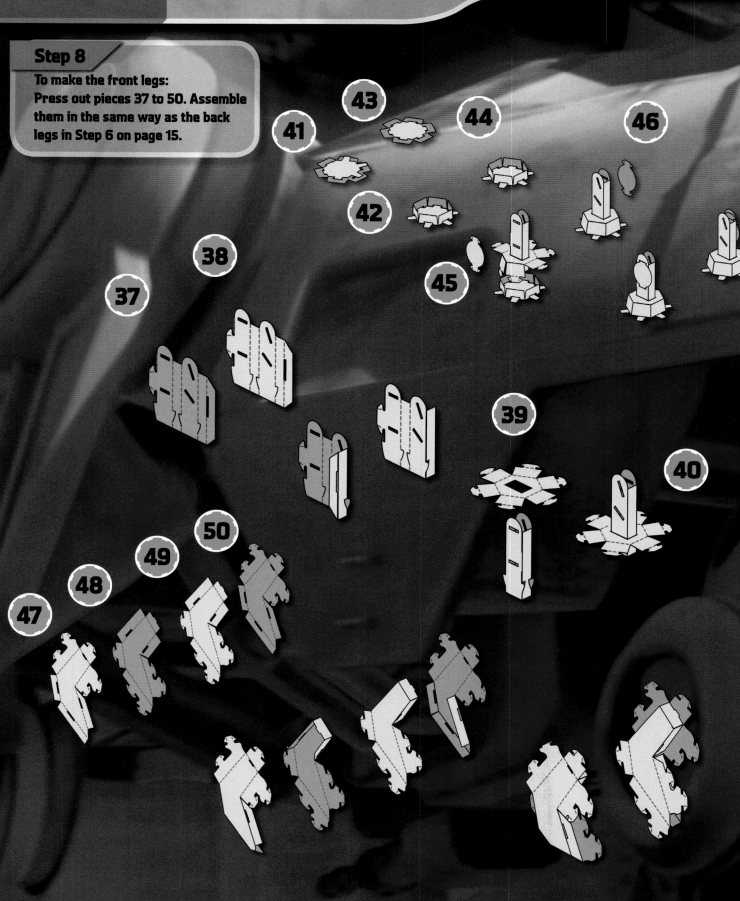

Step 8 (continued)

Step 9

Press out piece 51. This forms the front axle. Fold it up as shown and plug it into the front of the body section, using the six tabs (three on either side) as per the back axle. The notch on the bottom goes toward the back of the walker.

51

Step 10

To make the bulkheads:
Press out pieces 52 and 53, which form the left and right rear bulkheads. Then press out pieces 54 and 55, which form the left and right front bulkheads. Attach them to the body using the two tabs on each one.

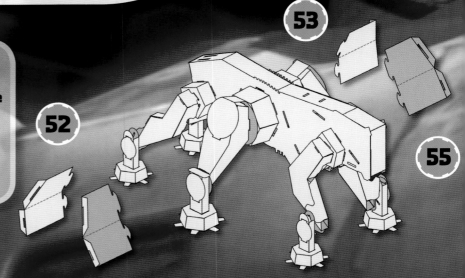

Step 11

To make the rear shell:
a. Press out pieces 56 to 58 and push the tabs from pieces 57 and 58 through the two middle slots on the back of piece 56.
b. Position the rear shell on the back of the body and push the same tabs through the two slots on the back of the walker. Pieces 57 and 58 will hold the shell in place.
c. Bend pieces 57 and 58 over into a half-box shape and push in their remaining tabs, so that they form two humps on the back of the shell.

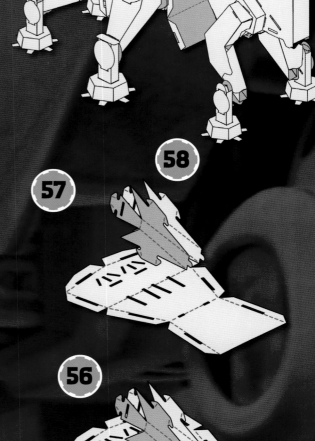

d. Press out piece 59. This will complete the rear shell. First, attach it to the rear of piece 56. Bend the sides around and secure them to the edges of piece 56. Then, secure the remaining tabs to the bulkhead pieces.

e. Finally, flip the two pieces protruding out the back inward and fasten them in place to form the rear of the walker.

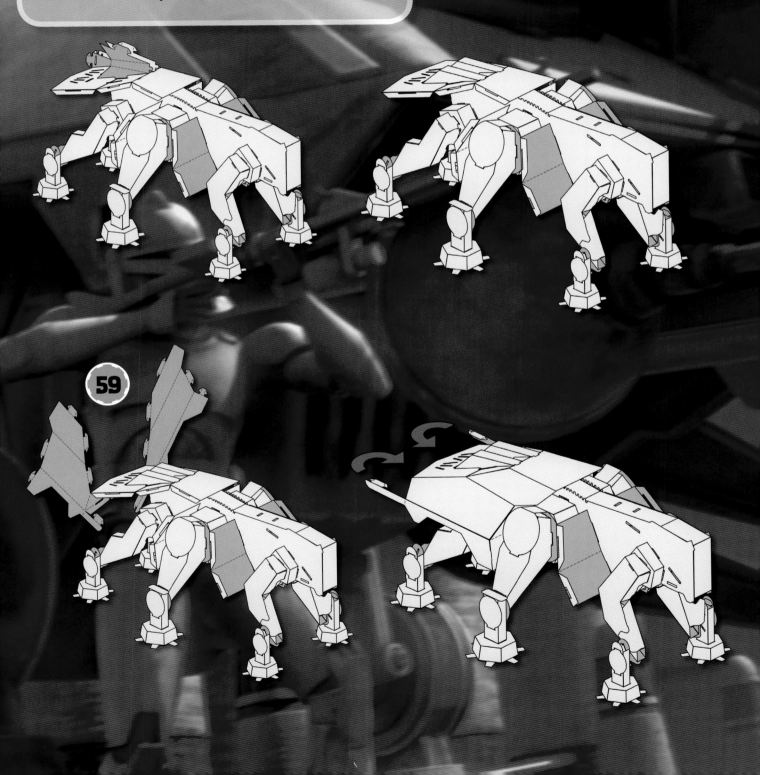

59

Step 12

To make the front shell:

a. Press out piece 60. Find the tongue between the two halves of the shell and slot it onto the top of the body in the middle.

b. Slot in the first two tabs on either side of the body.

c. Push in the second two tabs, securing the shell to the body.

d. Connect the shell to the front of the bulkheads.

e. You will be left with two flaps sticking out in front of the walker. Turn the walker over onto its back and fold these flaps under the shell section, putting the remaining tabs into the appropriate slots.

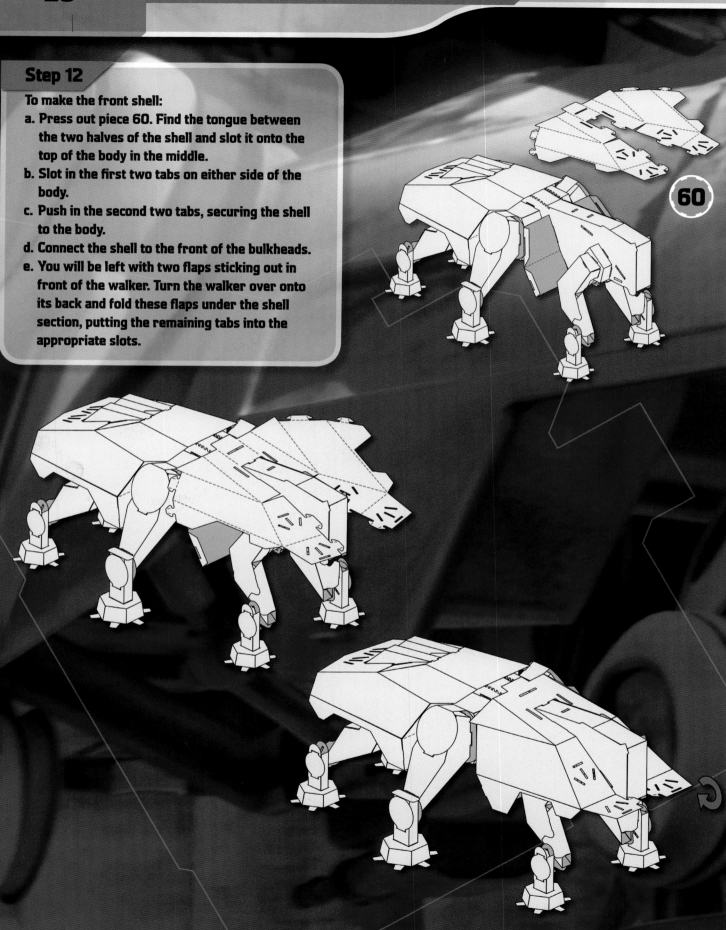

60

AT-TE WALKER

Step 13

To make the large gun turret:

a. Press out pieces 61 to 64.

b. Connect piece 61 to piece 62 using the little tab in the center of 62.

c. Fold the sides of piece 62 down to form the cannon.

d. Lever the cannon section down and connect the two side tabs so the cannon points forward.

e. Bend pieces 63 and 64 into shape, as shown.

f. Attach piece 63 to the top of the cannon and then attach piece 64.

g. Bend the rest of the gun turret into shape and attach it to the top of the front shell.

64

63

62

61

Step 14

To make the small gun turrets:
Press out pieces 65 to 70 and attach them by pushing
the tabs into the slots, as per the diagram. Don't worry
if they do not stand up at this point.

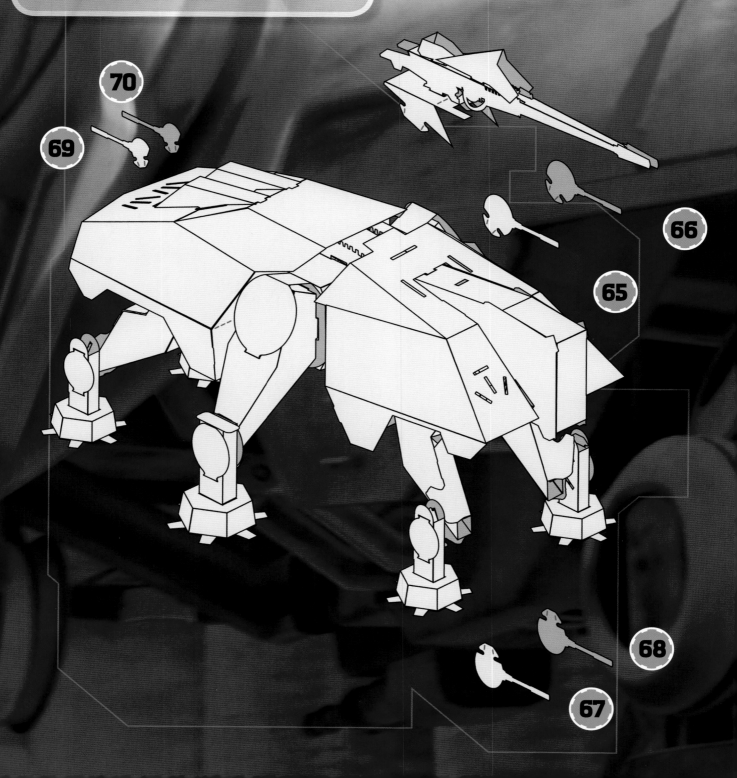

Step 15

To make the domes for the small gun turrets:

a. Press out pieces 71 to 76.

b. Bend the three leaves on each of the pieces below into a dome-like shape.

c. One by one, push the tabs on the domes over the gun turrets into the slots on the body. Start with the tab at the back of each gun. Then, stand the guns up straight and push in the front two tabs of the dome. The domes will hold the guns upright.

76

72

71

75

74

73

Congratulations! You have successfully completed the ultimate Jedi Master level for your model-making mission!

FINISHED MODELS

FINISHED MODELS